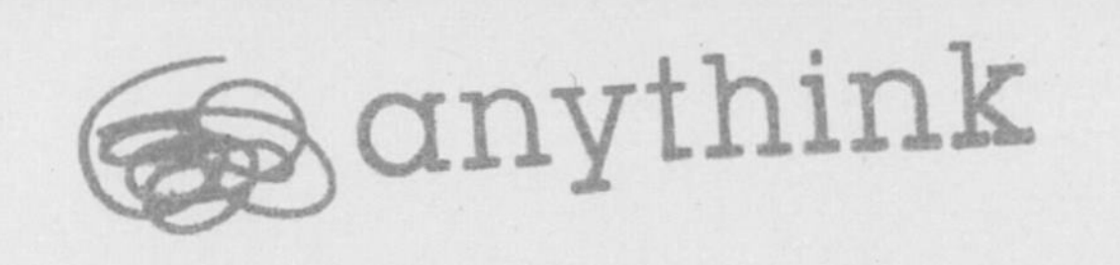

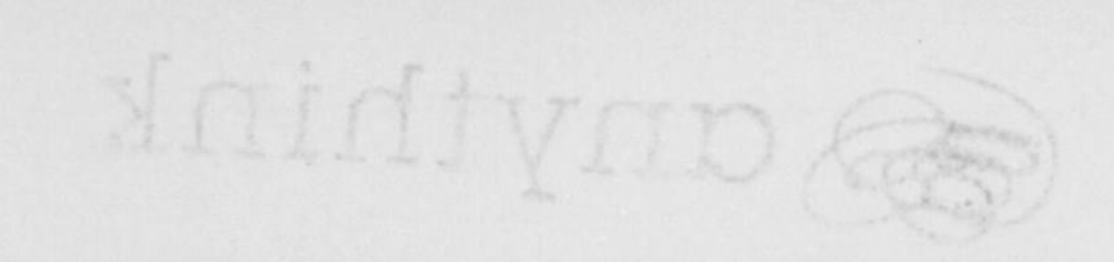

THAT STINKS!

To Rose, Simone, Andrew, Nathan, and David, who show and tell me great things every day
—A. K.

For Alice. I'll bet she would never bring anything stinky to show-and-tell, though.
—S. G.

SIMON & SCHUSTER BOOKS FOR YOUNG READERS
An imprint of Simon & Schuster Children's Publishing Division
1230 Avenue of the Americas, New York, New York 10020

Book design by Laurent Linn
The text for this book is set in Billy Std.
The illustrations for this book are rendered digitally.
Manufactured in China
0416 SCP
2 4 6 8 10 9 7 5 3 1
Library of Congress Cataloging-in-Publication Data
Katz, Alan.
That stinks! : a punny show-and-tell / Alan Katz ; illustrated by Stephen Gilpin. — First edition.
pages cm
Summary: Show-and-tell in Mrs. Mueller's classroom is full of wordplay—though not intentionally.
ISBN 978-1-4169-7880-0 (hardcover) — ISBN 978-1-4814-5145-1 (ebook)
[1. Show-and-tell presentations—Fiction. 2. Schools—Fiction. 3. Puns and punning—Fiction. 4. Humorous stories.]
I. Gilpin, Stephen, illustrator. II. Title.
PZ7.K15669Th 2016
[E]—dc23
2015000717

A Punny Show-and-Tell

Alan Katz

ILLUSTRATED BY

Stephen Gilpin

SIMON & SCHUSTER BOOKS FOR YOUNG READERS

NEW YORK LONDON TORONTO SYDNEY NEW DELHI

"It's too cold and rainy for outdoor recess," Mrs. Mueller told her class. "How about we stay inside and have show-and-tell instead?"

"That stinks!"
exclaimed Jimmy.

The class gasped.

"It's my pet skunk, Harry!
He **really** stinks!"

"Aw, nuts!"
said Susie.

"Pecans, almonds,
and walnuts.
Yum!"

"This totally bites!"
Mike announced.

"It's a tarantula . . . so **be careful!**"

"Incredibly cheesy!"
said Angela.

"Limburger cheese. **P-U!**"

"Gross!"
Monica said.

"I have 144 pencils. And 144 of **anything** equals one gross!"

"Garbage!"
Andrew said.

"I had nothing to bring, so here's
my family's dinner garbage!"

"This is screwed up!"
said Jeremy.

"It's the bulb that goes in my ceiling lamp—it gets screwed up!"

"Shocking!
Just shocking!"
Thomas told the group.

“This is an electric circuit. Never touch the red and black wires together!”

"Rotten!
Absolutely rotten!"
said Ellen.

"When you leave a banana inside your desk for a week, this is what happens!"

"This is the pits!"
Jordan said.

“They’re from avocados that grow on my family’s tree!”

"Boys and girls, I think this has been an excellent session of show-and-tell. Let's review. . . .

"That stinks, that's nuts, this bites, that's cheesy, that's gross, this is garbage, this is screwed up, that's shocking, that's absolutely rotten, and this is the pits!"

The class applauded.

But the principal had been watching.

Suddenly he yelled,

"I have had enough!"

"And it's all delicious!"